Read all the Ninja Meerkats adventures!

NINJA MEERKATS

THE ULTIMATE DRAGON WARRIOR

GARETH P. JONES

SQUARE
FISH

NEW YORK

SQUARE
FISH

An Imprint of Macmillan
175 Fifth Avenue
New York, NY 10010
mackids.com

Square Fish books may be purchased for business or promotional use.
For information on bulk purchases, please contact the Macmillan Corporate
and Premium Sales Department at (800) 221-7945 x5442
or by e-mail at specialmarkets@macmillan.com.

Library of Congress Cataloging-in-Publication Data Available
ISBN 978-1-250-04665-9 (paperback) / ISBN 978-1-250-04942-1 (e-book)

Originally published in Great Britain by Stripes Publishing
First Square Fish Edition: 2014
Square Fish logo designed by Filomena Tuosto

10 9 8 7 6 5 4 3 2 1

For Lucas, Flynn, and
Astrid Bousfield
~ *G P J*

Ah, it's you. Yes, I thought it would be. How did I know? Well, I am blessed with a kind of sixth sense. Unfortunately my other five senses appear to be letting me down in old age. Only yesterday I had a rather long chat with a lampshade. I found the conversation most illuminating. It turned out we both had a lot in common—each of us requires sixty watts. Since my hearing worsened, I'm forever asking, *What did you say? What was that? What's going on?* But that is neither here nor there. You don't want to hear about my problems.

What I should really be telling you about is the Clan of the Scorpion. Armed to the teeth with ninja-know-how, these four formidable fighters have just one goal—to keep the world safe from their sworn enemy, the Ringmaster and his villainous circus troupe.

Jet Flashfeet: a super-fast ninja whose only fault is craving the glory he so richly deserves.

Bruce "the muscle" Willowhammer: the strongest of the gang, though in the brain race he lags somewhat behind.

Donnie Dragonjab: a brilliant mind, inventor, and master of gadgets.

Chuck Cobracrusher: his clear leadership has saved the others' skins more times than I care to remember.

Oh, and me, Grandmaster One-Eye: as old and wise as the sand dunes themselves.

This story is one of my favorites, for it tells of how the clan took part in the

Trials of Dragon Island, competing for the title of Ultimate Dragon Warrior.

All of which reminds me of a poem on the subject of competitions by the snail poet, Mo Bilome.

> *In every competition*
> *In which I did compete,*
> *I always tried so hard to win*
> *But always faced defeat—*
> *I wonder if it's down*
> *To having so few feet.*

Anyway, I think it's time to get on with the story of . . .

THE ULTIMATE DRAGON WARRIOR.

CHAPTER ONE

DRAGON ISLAND

Two fishermen stood on the beach, watching the rowing boat make its way out to sea.

"Where do you think it's going?" asked one of the men.

"Looks like it's heading for Dragon Island," replied the other, pointing to an ominous-looking island with a huge volcano at its center, sending out red smoke into the sky.

"My cousin told me the island's named for the dragon smoke that billows from its center," said the first fisherman.

"Your cousin is a superstitious fool," said the other. "The smoke comes from the volcano."

"So why does it turn red every five years?"

"No one knows. I even swam to the island as a boy to try to find out, but there's nothing there other than wild lemurs."

Had the two fishermen seen the boat up close, they would have realized that the rower was a shop dummy, disguised as a fisherman. It was being operated by a remote control held by one of four ninja meerkats onboard.

"Another brilliant disguise, Donnie," said
Chuck.

"Thanks," replied Donnie. "I call it the
M.O.R.B.—Mannequin Operated Rowing
Boat."

"Why do we need a disguise anyway?"
asked Bruce.

"The invitation said we should arrive in
secret," replied Chuck.

"The invitation for me to be crowned
the Ultimate Dragon Warrior," added Jet.
"Ninja-boom!" He leaped up and punched
the air.

"Jet," shouted Donnie. "You're rocking—"

"You're right," Jet interrupted. "Being
invited to compete in the most awesome
kung-fu contest in the world *is* rocking,
isn't it?"

"I mean, you're rocking the boat," said
Donnie. "Besides, the invitation was for all

of us. Any one of us could win."

"Ha! It's bound to be me," said Jet.

"Jet, boasting is not a good thing," said Chuck.

"Yeah, my uncle almost died when it happened to him," said Bruce.

"He died from boasting?" asked Donnie.

"Yep," said Bruce. "It turned out he was allergic."

"I believe that was a bee sting, Bruce," said Chuck. "And actually, it could be that *none* of us takes home the title. Remember, the invitation said there would be eight competitors in total."

"I'll see off the competition with my Super-charged Shock Attack!" said Jet.

"What's that?" asked Bruce.

"It's my new move," explained Jet. "You rub your feet on the ground and charge yourself up with static electricity, then use

it to shock your opponent."

Donnie smirked. "If you want to shock them, just tell them how long you spent looking in the mirror this morning."

As the boat got closer to the island, the red smoke from the volcano blocked out the sun and threw the boat into the shadow of the island.

"Donnie, what did your background check reveal about this island?" asked Chuck.

"Very little," replied Donnie. "It's named Dragon Island because of the red smoke, but everything else is a mystery."

"Ooh, spooky," said Bruce.

"Are we sure this isn't one of the Ringmaster's traps?" asked Chuck. "A strange invitation, a remote island— I wouldn't put it past him."

"No way," said Jet. "The Trials of Dragon Island are legendary. Once every five years, when the volcano smoke turns red, the world's finest martial arts fighters are summoned to compete for the title of Ultimate Dragon Warrior."

The boat drew close to the island, giving the meerkats a good view of the white sand on the beaches that surrounded it. Donnie pressed a button on his remote control that stopped the dummy rowing.

"Why are we stopping?" asked Bruce. "We're not there yet."

"The invitation said there should be no evidence of visitors on the island," replied Donnie. "So we need to leave the boat here. It's time for the M.O.R.B. to go fishing."

He pressed another button and the dummy pulled in the oars and picked up a fishing rod. The other meerkats watched in amazement as the dummy cast the line out to sea.

"The hook on the end will latch on to the ocean floor and act as an anchor, so the boat doesn't float away," said Donnie.

"Very clever," said Chuck.

"So we've got to swim to the island?" said Jet, aghast.

"Don't worry," said Donnie. "You won't have to mess your fur up."

From his backpack, Donnie pulled out four clear plastic bags and handed them to the others. He then showed them how to climb inside and seal the entrance.

"This is weird," said Bruce.

"Yeah, I feel like I've been shrink-wrapped," remarked Jet.

"There's a red toggle inside. Pull it, like this," said Donnie. He demonstrated and suddenly his plastic bag inflated into a clear ball around him. The others did the same.

"I call them Ninja-zorbs," said Donnie.

"Now I feel like a hamster," said Jet.

"Yes, they work in the same way as hamster balls. Watch."

Donnie ran forward, propelling the clear ball over the top of the boat and onto the surface of the water. The others followed and soon they were all charging toward the island.

"Donnie, the brilliance of your inventions never ceases to amaze me," said Chuck.

"I've heard of running water," said Bruce. "But we're running *on* water."

The Clan of the Scorpion reached the beach and began deflating the Ninja-zorbs.

"Very impressive," said a voice.

"Yeah, it was all right, I suppose," said another.

They turned to find a pelican and a badger standing behind them.

CHAPTER TWO

EMPRESS ME

The pelican, who wore a yellow bandana tied around his head, bowed respectfully, while the badger, who wore a black robe with a white belt, stood with his arms crossed.

"You must be the other contestants," said Chuck, returning the pelican's bow. "We are the Clan of the Scorpion."

"It's an honor to meet you," said the pelican.

"And it'll be a pleasure to *beat* you," added the badger, with a chuckle.

"I'd like to see you try," said Bruce, squaring up to him.

The badger laughed. "The name's Mickey 'knock out' Stripes. My fans call me Stripes."

"Fans?" scoffed Jet.

"Yep. You are lucky enough to be talking to the undefeated winner of the Interspecies Wrestling Competition, the No-Holds-Barred Championships, and the Tooth 'n' Claw Caged Fighter of the Year three years running. I put the *bad* into *bad*ger." He boxed the air. "A quick one-two, and you novices will be out cold."

"We certainly are novices when it comes

to competition fighting," said Chuck. "We are more used to the real thing."

The pelican spoke. "All of us have good reason to be here. Mr. Stripes was just telling me how his father competed in the last competition, five years ago."

"Yeah," said Stripes. "The difference is that my old man didn't win, whereas I will."

"A wise warrior is always prepared for battle. A foolish one expects victory," said the pelican.

"I couldn't have put it better myself," said Chuck.

The pelican bowed again. "I am sorry, I haven't introduced myself. My name is Plato."

"I *knew* I recognized you," Jet said excitedly. "You're Plato Wynn, the high-kicking pelican. I read an interview with you in *The Karate Times*. It said that you once kicked an opponent so hard, he went into orbit around the planet."

"That's him all right," said Stripes. "Watch." He punched the trunk of a nearby palm tree, causing a coconut to fall. It would have whacked Plato on the head, but the pelican jumped into the air, spun around, and kicked the coconut away, sending it soaring so high into the sky that it reached a passing cloud.

"Astounding," said Chuck.

"High praise indeed from Chuck Cobracrusher."

"You know my name?" said Chuck.

"Your abilities are legendary," said the pelican. "Chuck Cobracrusher, wise leader of the Clan of the Scorpion. Your companions are also well known to me. Jet Flashfeet, the super-fast ninja always on the lookout for a new move, Bruce 'the force' Willowhammer, as strong as ten lions, and Donnie Dragonjab, the inventor of many brilliant gadgets and dumbfounding disguises. Your reputations precede you. Now we are only waiting for the eighth competitor."

"The eighth?" said Donnie. "I only count six of us here."

"You are not the first person to overlook Lay-Z." Plato pointed out a mound of fur lying in the shade of the palm tree.

The meerkats took a
closer look and saw
that it was a furry
creature, curled up
and fast asleep.

"Wow," said Jet. "Lay-Z,
the three-toed sloth, famous for inventing
the martial arts style known as Do Zing.
I can't believe I'm here alongside my
heroes!"

"Thanks," said Stripes.

"I didn't mean you," snapped Jet.

Bruce looked up. "Hey, look—the
coconut's falling back to earth."

Donnie squinted at the sky. "That's no
coconut."

"How can you tell?" asked Bruce.

"Because it's dressed in an orange robe
and has just opened a parachute. Someone
must have jumped from that plane."

"Hey," said Bruce, peering more closely at the figure suspended from a parachute. "It's one of the Shaolin Monkeys."

The spiky-haired monkey detached his parachute just before he hit the ground, and landed in an elegant forward roll. He sprang to his feet and joined the others.

"It's Turbold," said Jet, who had fought both against and alongside the monkey back in India.

"Well, well, well, if it isn't the Clan of the Scorpion! I wondered if you would be here," said Turbold, grinning. "When does this competition start?"

"I think we're about to find out," said Chuck. "Listen."

From the jungle behind them they could hear sounds that grew louder and louder, until finally the source of the noise was revealed.

Out of the jungle emerged hundreds of lemurs dressed in plain white robes. Some of them banged drums made from coconuts. Some played trumpets made from bamboo. Others held big branches, which they used as fans.

At the center of this troupe was a great wooden carriage, pulled along by more lemurs. Sitting on top was a female lemur who wore a golden robe and a magnificent headdress with a ruby at its center. She held up a paw and the music stopped.

"We extend a warm welcome to the contestants hoping to become the Ultimate Dragon Warrior," she said.

All the contestants bowed, except for Stripes, who nodded his head in greeting, and Lay-Z, who was still fast asleep.

"We are Empress Me," said the lemur.

"All of you?" said Bruce.

"No, just us," she replied, pointing to herself. "These are our loyal subjects." She indicated the other lemurs.

"Why's she speaking like that?" asked Bruce out of the corner of his mouth.

"It's how royal people speak, Bruce," responded Chuck quietly. "She's an empress."

"Well, she don't *empress* me much," whispered Donnie.

"It's a great honor to be here," said Chuck.

"The honor is all ours, Mr. Cobracrusher. You have been selected as the eight finest kung-fu fighters in the world, and yet there can only be one Ultimate Dragon Warrior."

"It's definitely going to be me," said Jet.

"Yeah, right," said Turbold and Stripes together.

"The competition will begin shortly. You will learn some of our greatest secrets during your stay, so now we ask that you swear an oath of secrecy. Please raise your hands."

The contestants did as they were told. Even Lay-Z raised a long, clawed hand, although the sloth kept his eyes shut.

"Now, repeat after us," said Empress Me. "We swear, on all that we hold dear and precious, to keep the secrets of Dragon Island."

They all repeated these words: "During

our stay we will have no contact with the outside world. If we break this oath, we accept the consequences."

The contestants lowered their hands.

"What about that lot?" said Stripes, pointing at the crowd of lemurs. "They all keep your secrets, do they?"

"Our loyal subjects took a vow of silence many years ago. Here, we dedicate every moment to the study of martial arts. The lemurs of Dragon Island live and breathe kung fu."

"What do you eat?" asked Bruce. "My stomach's been growling like a grizzly bear with a bellyache since I left the mainland."

Empress Me smiled. "We will show you, Mr. Willowhammer. We have a special banquet prepared."

"A banquet," said Bruce. "Now you're talking."

CHAPTER THREE

DRAWING LOTS

Surrounded by hundreds of silent lemurs, the contestants followed Empress Me's carriage. They made their way through dense jungle, where the sunlight was blocked by the large-leafed vegetation, and brightly colored birds perched in the trees.

They walked by the side of a trickling stream to a clearing where a fantastic banquet had been laid out on a long table carved from the trunk of a fallen tree. There were eight seats around the table and a huge wooden throne at the end.

Empress Me stepped down from her carriage and took her place at the head of the table.

"You should all find something to eat here," she said. "For Plato, there are seven types of freshly caught fish. For Turbold, a variety of local nuts have been specially picked. For Lay-Z, there is a bowl of leaves, and for the meerkats, a selection of bugs and lizards. Stripes, as badgers are omnivorous, you may take your pick."

"What does om-niv-or-ous mean?" asked Bruce.

"It means you'll eat anything," said Donnie.

"So I'm omnivorous too?" said Bruce. "Because I eat anything."

"You eat *everything*," said Donnie. "That's just greedy."

Chuck took a seat next to Plato, and

Donnie and Turbold sat opposite. Bruce sat down at the end of the table by Lay-Z, who had been carefully placed on a chair, still fast asleep. Jet found himself facing Stripes.

"Hey, Jet," said Turbold. "How would you like your egg cooked?"

"What egg?" asked Jet, puzzled by the question.

"The one that's going to be on your face when you lose," Turbold replied with a smirk.

"Well, you'd better leave some room for humble pie when I defeat you," replied Jet.

"Ha! On the contrary, you're the one who'll be eating your words," Turbold retaliated.

"I wish you two would take a vow of silence," Chuck said.

"So, tell me, Empress," said Stripes, speaking with his mouth full of food. "What is the prize for this competition?"

"There is no prize money," she replied. "The victor will be named the Ultimate Dragon Warrior. This is a great honor."

"No prize money?" blurted out Stripes, spraying bits of food from his mouth. "Even those tight-fisted fellows at the Worldwide Wildlife Wrestling Foundation offer prize money to the winner."

"We realize that you are used to fighting in more conventional competitions, Mr. Stripes. Like your father before you, you have earned a place here, but as you have seen, we live in isolation on this island," said Empress Me. "We have no need for money."

Stripes grabbed another handful of nuts. "Suppose I'd better make the most of the free grub then, hadn't I?"

Everyone else happily ate and drank while speculating about the upcoming event and telling tales of past triumphs. Then Empress Me stood, clapped her hands, and addressed the whole table.

"It now falls to us to explain how the trials will work," she said. "There will be three trials in total, over as many days. The first will reveal the warrior with the greatest fighting skills, the second will show the warrior with the greatest endurance. Only the winners of these two trials will go through to the final trial and have a chance to be crowned the Ultimate Dragon Warrior."

A buzz of excited chatter spread around the table.

"So we fight first?" said Jet. "Brilliant!"

"I could take on all of you blindfolded," boasted Stripes.

"The fighting trial consists of three knock-out rounds," continued Empress Me. "You will all be assigned an opponent in Round One. The four winners of Round One will go through to Round Two. The two winners of the second round will fight in the final."

"Great. Knocking out is what I do best," said Stripes.

"You are not in one of your caged fights now," said Empress Me. "There is no need to knock anyone out. The victor must land three strikes on his opponent. They needn't be hard, for the Ultimate Dragon Warrior will be as merciful as he is strong and agile. We will now draw your names from this bowl, to see who will fight who in Round One."

A lemur came forward, holding up a beautifully carved wooden bowl. Empress Me reached into the bowl and pulled out two pieces of paper.

"Chuck will fight Lay-Z," she announced.

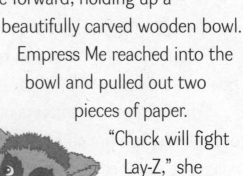

"If he ever wakes up," said Donnie.

The others turned to look at the sloth. He was still fast asleep, although the leaves that had been placed in his bowl had mysteriously disappeared.

Empress Me pulled out two more bits of paper. "Turbold will fight Donnie," she proclaimed.

"Easy!" said Turbold.

"We'll see," said Donnie. "I'm packing a few surprises in here." He tapped his backpack confidently.

"We are afraid not, Donnie," said Empress Me. "No weaponry of any kind is allowed in these fights. That goes for everyone. No nunchucks, swords, or gadgets. The Ultimate Dragon Warrior will rely on his own wit and fighting skills."

"Let's see how you fare without your famous gadgets," said Turbold, with a defiant grin at Donnie.

Empress Me plucked out the next two names. "Stripes will fight Plato," she said.

Stripes snorted. "You'll be picking up the bill once I've finished with you," he said. "Picking it up off the floor, that is."

"Hold on," said Jet. "That means I'm fighting Bruce."

"Correct," said Empress Me.

"But . . . we're always on the same team," said Bruce.

"Not this time," said Empress Me. "Now, it grows late. Our subjects will show you to your sleeping quarters. We lemurs are tree-dwellers like Turbold and Lay-Z, but there is a shelter for Plato, a den for Stripes, and a burrow for the Clan of the Scorpion. We hope you all get a good night's sleep, for you will need your energy tomorrow."

CHAPTER FOUR

THE TRIAL OF COMBAT

The next morning, everyone enjoyed a lavish breakfast. Then the contestants were led to another clearing at the foot of the great volcano, where they could see the red smoke drifting up into the blue sky.

A fighting ring had been marked out with sticks and to one side was a large golden gong. In the surrounding trees, hundreds of lemurs sat and applauded as the contestants arrived. Stripes held up a paw in thanks, as though the applause was all for him. Lay-Z was carried into position by two lemurs.

A fanfare of bamboo trumpets announced the arrival of Empress Me. She was seated on top of a huge leaf carried by four lemurs. She waited for the applause to die down, then spoke.

"Welcome to the Fighting Trial of Dragon Island." The lemurs applauded wildly. "We want good clean fights," continued Empress Me. "The aim is to win, not to cause injury." She looked at Stripes as she said this. "Round One will involve four battles. First, Chuck Cobracrusher versus Lay-Z."

Chuck laid down his sword and entered the ring.

"Good luck, Chuck," shouted Jet.

"Go get him," added Donnie.

Lay-Z didn't stir. Two lemurs carried the sleeping sloth into the ring and placed him on the ground. Another lemur sounded the huge gong. "Let the fight commence," Empress Me commanded.

Chuck bowed. Lay-Z didn't move.

Chuck assumed an attack position, with his legs bent, his right arm out straight, and his left raised in the air.

Lay-Z let out a small snore.

"I've never seen Do Zing in action before," said Jet excitedly.

"It's thrilling to watch so far," Donnie yawned.

Chuck approached slowly. Then, suddenly, Lay-Z's eyes shot open. Chuck attacked but the sloth rolled out of the way, leaped up, and caught him on the chin, sending him reeling.

"One point to Lay-Z," announced Empress Me.

The lemurs applauded.

Chuck was quick to retaliate and make it one–all. The fight picked up speed now, as Chuck and Lay-Z blocked and attacked each other's moves at great speed, each scoring another point to make it two–all. Then Chuck moved swiftly and won the fight with a perfectly executed roundhouse kick that floored his opponent.

"Chuck Cobracrusher wins," cried Empress Me.

Lay-Z bowed to Chuck, walked to the ringside, and immediately fell fast asleep.

Empress Me announced that Donnie and Turbold were next up. Donnie took off his backpack and followed the monkey into the ring. Donnie was first to get the advantage, sending Turbold staggering back with a kick to the chest. Turbold retaliated with a flying attack, which missed Donnie, but distracted him long enough for Turbold to roll along the ground, spring up, and tap him on the back, making it even. After two more battles the score was two–all but, in a dramatic finish, Turbold sprang up, spun around, did a triple somersault, and clipped Donnie on the head to win the fight.

"Turbold wins," announced Empress Me.

"You fought with great honor," said Chuck, as Donnie rejoined him.

"Really? I thought I was fighting with Turbold," replied Donnie, taking his defeat in good spirit.

"Next up, Plato and Stripes," yelled Empress Me.

After the gong sounded, Stripes showed that he was certainly strong. But he was not fast enough for the pelican. Plato was a sublime fighter. With perfect poise, he anticipated his opponent's every move. The badger failed to even land one punch, and Plato won three–nil, finishing Stripes off with a left-footed high kick that sent him flying into a tree trunk. Several lemurs tumbled down from the branches above.

"Looks like Stripes is seeing stars," said Donnie.

Stripes got up, brushed himself down, and grumpily stomped back to the sidelines.

Empress Me announced the final fight of Round One. "Bruce versus Jet!"

"I'll go easy on you," said Jet, walking into the fighting ring.

"And I'll try not to mess up your fur," replied Bruce.

The two meerkats had sparred many times before, but, once the gong had sounded, it was different. This was serious.

Jet got the first strike in, landing a tickle-punch on Bruce's shoulder.

"One point to Jet," said Empress Me.

"I didn't even feel that," exclaimed Bruce.

"Let's see if you feel this," replied Jet. He did a figure-of-eight leap then ducked into a forward roll, pounced, and landed a twisting punch on Bruce's stomach.

"Another point to Jet," cried Empress Me.

Bruce yelled out in annoyance. "Right, that's it," he said, charging forward. His speed took Jet by surprise and Bruce knocked him clean off his feet, scoring his first point.

"I didn't hit you that hard!" cried Jet.

The two meerkats circled each other, maintaining constant eye contact.

Suddenly, Bruce lunged forward, but Jet dodged and caught his friend on the shoulder with his tail.

"Jet wins," the empress announced.

"Ninja-boom!" Jet cried.

The lemurs applauded wildly until Empress Me held up a paw. "The winners of Round One are through to Round Two. Chuck will go up against Turbold, followed by Jet and Plato."

Chuck and Turbold were evenly matched. Both competitors were spinning, jumping, dodging, ducking, and diving to avoid the other's attacks. It wasn't long before both Chuck and Turbold had two points each.

They stood face-to-face, breathing heavily and observing each other carefully, when suddenly, a cell phone beeped.

"Sorry," said Stripes, pulling a phone from his belt.

Turbold took advantage of the distraction. He flipped up on his paws and swung his tail, clipping Chuck on the top of his head.

"That's not fair," shouted Jet.

"Yeah, he was distracted," added Donnie.

Empress Me turned angrily to Stripes. "There should be no contact with the outside world on Dragon Island."

"I thought I'd turned it off," said Stripes defensively.

She addressed Chuck. "Would you like to replay the point? It was an unfair distraction."

"We both heard it," said Chuck. "But only I was distracted. Therefore Turbold is the rightful winner."

Turbold and Chuck bowed to one another and returned to the sidelines.

"Next up, Jet versus Plato. The winner will fight Turbold in the final round," Empress Me announced. "And Mr. Stripes, please ensure your phone is now off."

Stripes mumbled something under his breath but switched off his phone.

"Good luck, Jet," said Chuck.

Jet took his place in the ring opposite Plato, but when Empress Me announced the beginning of the fight and the gong sounded, neither of the competitors moved.

"What's going on?" asked Bruce.

"Neither wants to give anything away by making the first attack," Chuck replied.

When they finally moved, it was

impossible to say who went first. The fight
was like an elegant dance that resulted in Jet
landing a soft tap on the pelican's bill. Plato
quickly responded with a right-footed kick.
Before Jet recovered he was caught again by
the edge of the bird's webbed foot and sent
flying. Finally, Jet took control. He ducked a
series of rapid kicks and scored a point with
a quick return kick. He then somersaulted
over Plato's head, tapping him on his bill.

"Jet wins!" yelled Empress Me.

Plato bowed low. "It is an
honor to lose to such a worthy
opponent."

"Final round," announced Empress Me. "Jet versus Turbold. Jet, would you like a rest first?"

"No way," said Jet. "I'm just getting warmed up."

The lemurs applauded in excitement. Turbold and Jet bowed and the gong sounded.

"I have beaten Chuck and Donnie," said Turbold. "You'll be a piece of cake."

"I think you'll find I've got the recipe for victory," replied Jet.

"Ha! You don't even have the ingredients," countered Turbold.

Over on the sideline, Donnie sighed. "Always with the cheesy battle banter, those two."

"All this talk of cake and cheese is making me hungry," said Bruce.

Once the gong had sounded, Turbold

made the first move. It was a high-flying
kick. Jet dodged it, then rallied with a series
of punches and kicks that completely missed
their target. The two competitors were so
well-matched that they fought for some time
without either scoring a single point, but
eventually the tip of Jet's tail connected with
Turbold's stomach and he won the first
point. This made Turbold up his game—he
took Jet by surprise with a spectacular
double backflip, and equalized. Two more
fantastic bouts made it two-all.

"Trial point," cried Empress Me. "The next
competitor to score will win the first trial."

"Get him, Jet!" cried Donnie.

"Quiet, please." Empress Me glared at
Donnie.

Turbold and Jet eyed each other while
Jet subtly rubbed his feet on the ground.

"What's he doing?" whispered Bruce.

"The Super-charged Shock Attack,"
mouthed Chuck.

Sure enough, Jet's fur was soon
standing on end. When Turbold lunged, Jet
aimed an outstretched paw at him. A spark
of blue light flew across the ring at Turbold,
sending the monkey staggering backwards.

Jet seized the moment and leaped forward, tapping Turbold lightly on the nose—and giving him a second shock.

"Point to Jet," cried Empress Me. "Jet wins the first trial."

"Ninja-boooooooom!" cried Jet, punching the air.

The lemurs applauded and Bruce charged forward to congratulate him.

"Bruce, no!" shouted Chuck.

But it was too late. Bruce threw his arms around Jet. There was an almighty flash of light, and Bruce flew backwards through the air into a tree trunk.

"Shocking," said Donnie with a smirk.

CHAPTER FIVE

THE TRIAL OF THE TEA TREE

That evening over dinner, the hot topic of
conversation was Jet's spectacular victory
and what the following day's trial might
involve. Empress Me, however, would give no
hints as to what it might be. The feast was
even more lavish than the previous night. Jet
and Turbold were happily goading each other
about who was the best, Bruce was stuffing
his face, and Chuck was talking to Plato
about philosophy. Even Stripes was getting
into the mood, wowing a group of lemurs
with his ability to juggle six grapefruits.

"Where did you learn to do that?" asked Donnie.

"I'm not only the best prize fighter the animal kingdom has ever known, you know," he replied. "I have many talents. What about you? Have you got any party tricks?"

"Have I got any party tricks?" echoed Donnie. "You bet I have."

Delving into his backpack, Donnie pulled out a long tube with a wick coming out of one end.

"What's that? A firework?" snorted Stripes.

"This is a ground-to-air, movement-sensitive, programmable missile," said Donnie. "It pinpoints its target and is powerful enough to blow a tank wide open."

"How is that a party trick?" asked Stripes.

"Because it also makes a brilliant firework. Watch this."

After breakfast the next morning, the competitors followed Empress Me's carriage on a trek across the island. As before, two lemurs carried Lay-Z, who was still fast asleep. They followed the stream until they came to a spot where it cascaded in a waterfall down to a pool below. By the side of the stream was a tree that had grown outward so that its twisting branches hung over the drop to the sparkling water.

The eight competitors gathered around as Empress Me climbed down from her carriage and stood in front of the tree. The army of lemurs settled around to watch. Behind them, rising up from the jungle was the volcano, sending out its endless line of red smoke.

"This second trial is a test of endurance,

focus, and resolve. It is known as . . ."
Empress Me paused for effect, then said,
"The Trial of the Tea Tree."

Stripes yawned. "Sounds thrilling."

"Once again, you must lay down your
weapons and gadgets before you take
part," commanded Empress Me.

Donnie, Chuck, and Jet did as she said.

"What do we have to do?" asked Plato.

A lemur stepped forward holding a tray
with eight cups of tea, each full to the brim.

"Each of you must take a cup of our
local tea. You must carry it to a branch of
your choosing and hold it without spilling
it. The competitor who holds it the longest
will be the winner."

"Sitting in a tree holding a cup of tea
isn't my idea of a trial," said Stripes, but he
still took the cup and carried it carefully
along one of the branches.

Secretly Jet agreed with him, but he said nothing and took the cup. Lay-Z opened his eyes long enough to get into position, then rested the tea on his stomach and went back to sleep. Soon all eight competitors were perched on branches, clutching or balancing cups.

"Let the trial begin," cried Empress Me.

After what seemed like hours, Jet was beginning to wonder whether the trial was really a test of who got bored first. Then, without warning, Donnie giggled.

"Hey! That tickles," he said, slapping his arm.

"What does?" asked Jet. But before Donnie could answer, Jet felt a tickling sensation start in his feet, then work its way slowly up his leg.

"What's going on?" he asked.

"Look, they're t-t-tickling ants," said Donnie, bursting into hysterical laughter and dropping his cup of tea. The liquid splashed out as the cup fell down into the water below.

"Donnie is out," cried Empress Me.

Donnie climbed back along the branch to the solid ground and picked up his backpack. "I'd have been all right if I'd been able to use my anti-tickle lotion," he said, as he put on his backpack.

Stripes and Plato were the next two competitors to dissolve into giggles and spill their tea, followed by Bruce, who dropped his cup and started licking his body.

"I didn't think you were ticklish," Donnie said.

"I'm not," said Bruce.

"So why did you move?"

Bruce licked his arm. "I was hungry. Ants are yummy."

There were four competitors remaining. Chuck, Jet, Turbold, and Lay-Z stayed dead still on their branches, watched by hundreds

of lemurs in the surrounding trees. Empress Me licked a finger and held it in the air. "Ah, the wind is changing direction. It is time for the next part of the trial."

The wind made the branches sway, making it more difficult for the remaining competitors to keep the teacups steady, but still none spilled a drop.

"Is that it? Ants and wind?" said Stripes.

"Don't knock it. The ants were enough to see *us* off," said Donnie.

"It is not the wind that will test them," said Empress Me. "Please, put these on."

A lemur stepped forward and handed out masks made from leaves and vines. Donnie, Bruce, Plato, and Stripes followed the lemurs' example and slipped them over their heads so that the leaf covered their mouths. Plato needed two masks to cover his large bill.

"What are these masks for?" asked Bruce.

"They will protect you from the effects of the smoke," said Empress Me.

"What smoke?" asked Donnie.

Empress Me replied by pointing to the volcano. The breeze had caught the red smoke and it was billowing down toward them. In seconds they were lost in a thick red mist. When the wind dropped and the smoke cleared, it revealed Lay-Z climbing back along the branch, without a cup of tea. When he reached the ground, he collapsed and fell back to sleep. The other contestants were still in their positions, but they were swaying from side to side.

"What's happening?" asked Donnie.

"The red smoke disorientates and confuses all who breathe it," explained Empress Me.

Out on his tree branch, Chuck was certainly beginning to feel disorientated. The world had started to spin, slowly at first, then faster and faster. He concentrated hard on not spilling the tea but then he spotted Jet lose his grip and fall from the branch. Without a thought Chuck dropped his cup, swung from the branch, and grabbed Jet's tail, pulling him back up and leading him to safety.

"Chuck and Jet are out," said Empress Me. "Turbold wins."

Hearing this, Turbold's concentration broke and he jerked suddenly. He would

have fallen down into the pool below had
Donnie not suddenly dived after him. He
pressed a button on the shoulder strap of
his backpack,
activating two
large wings which
popped out of the
sides. A second
button ignited an
afterburner,
propelling him
down toward
Turbold. He
grabbed the
falling monkey
then looped back
up and landed in
front of Empress Me.
The lemurs applauded
wildly.

"What's going on?" Turbold asked groggily.

"You won the trial," replied Donnie.

Jet was spinning around in circles, giggling and pointing up at the sky, saying, "The clouds are like candyfloss."

"So they are," said Turbold, looking up.

"There is something peculiar about them," Chuck said, swaying and smiling.

"They've all gone funny in the head," said Bruce.

"It is the effect of the smoke," said Empress Me, pulling the leaf mask from her face. "Now the smoke has cleared, they will be back to normal in a few minutes."

"Why does it have this effect?" asked Donnie. "And how do these masks work?"

"Duh," said Stripes. "They're made from the antidote leaf."

Empress Me turned to look at him.

"How can you know this?" she asked.

Stripes shifted uncomfortably. "Well, I mean it stands to reason, doesn't it?" he said. "These leaves must have some kind of antidote to whatever's in that smoke."

Donnie eyed him suspiciously, but Empress Me went on. "All will be revealed in the third and final trial. As Jet is the Champion of Combat and Turbold the Champion of Endurance, tomorrow they will face each other to decide who will be proclaimed the Ultimate Dragon Warrior."

"This is a stupid competition if you ask me," grumbled Stripes.

"No one did," said Plato. "Jet and Turbold are worthy finalists, both of them."

"Indeed they are, Plato," said Empress Me. "And tomorrow we will learn which of them will be the winner."

CHAPTER SIX

AN OVERHEARD CONVERSATION

After the evening meal, everyone returned to their sleeping quarters. Having eaten so much, Bruce was soon snoring, and it wasn't long before Chuck and Jet had also dropped off. Donnie, however, had difficulty getting to sleep, thinking about what Stripes had said. The badger seemed to know more about the mysterious effects of the red smoke than he was letting on.

After tossing and turning for a while, Donnie climbed out of the burrow and headed into the jungle. It was peaceful so late at night and all he could hear were the noises of the jungle. The trickling of the stream . . . The chirrups of crickets . . . The sound of a phone ringing . . .

Donnie stopped dead. *The sound of a phone ringing?* Stripes was the only competitor he had seen with a phone, but Empress Me had clearly told him to turn it off. Donnie crept closer and heard Stripes speaking quietly.

". . . I told you, we're not supposed to have our phones on. You don't want me to get thrown off the island, do you? You need me," the badger was saying.

Donnie wished he had his backpack
with him, where he kept a device that
would have enabled him to hear the other
side of the conversation. As it was, he could
only hear Stripes.

"Tomorrow is the final trial," continued
Stripes. "I didn't get through. . . . No, it's a
monkey and a meerkat."

There was a pause.

"Yeah, four of them," said Stripes. "They
call themselves the Clan of the Scorpion or
something. . . . No, wait for me. That way,
they can do all the hard work and we can
reap the benefits."

Stripes ended the phone call and
Donnie stepped out from his hiding place.
"Who were you speaking to?" he
demanded. "Why did you mention us?"

"Oh, what are you . . . ? I was . . ." Stripes
paused and then said, "I was talking to my

manager. He asked about you. He may be interested in signing you up. There's good money on the competition circuit."

"The Clan of the Scorpion fight for honor, not money. What did you mean about someone doing all the work and you reaping the benefits?"

"Er . . . well . . . My manager reckons he can still charge more for me to fight now I've competed in the prestigious Trials of Dragon Island."

Donnie eyed him suspiciously. Every answer Stripes gave was perfectly plausible, and yet Donnie didn't believe him.

"I'll see you in the morning," Stripes said, and they parted ways. Donnie needed more clues about what Stripes was up to—he would have to keep a close eye on him.

The next day, the contestants were led along a path that curled up toward the summit of the volcano. Donnie walked alongside Chuck. He glanced back at Stripes and said, "Last night I heard Stripes on his phone."

"He should be careful," replied Chuck. "Empress Me told him to turn it off."

"I couldn't tell exactly what he was talking about, but I don't trust him."

The procession continued up and up the volcano. Empress Me was carried on a banana leaf by a team of lemurs. They were walking for the whole morning. There was a magnificent panoramic view of the island and the twinkling ocean around it.

As they neared the mouth of the volcano, Empress Me signaled for the group to stop. She ordered several lemurs to hand out leaf masks. The contestants could feel the heat from the mouth of the volcano, where the red smoke was billowing out, up into the sky.

They kept climbing until they finally reached the summit. The army of lemurs gathered on the slopes and listened to Empress Me address the competitors.

"Yesterday you asked us why the red smoke had such an effect on those who inhaled it. The answer is this." She held up a dried flower with red petals. "It is our island's most precious secret," she said. "In the walls of this volcano are many caves. Inside one of these caves there grows this rare species of plant. It is known as Herbiscus Confusus and it flowers only once every five years.

"The red flower, when burned, produces a vapor capable of throwing all who inhale it into complete confusion. The swirling air currents from the volcano blow these flowers into the lava down inside the crater. The volcano burns the flowers and the smoke turns red. It was this red smoke that disorientated those in the tree yesterday.

"These masks are made from another rare plant that is also unique to this island,

known as the Clari-tree. Its leaves provide a natural antidote to the effects of the red smoke. These are the reasons why Dragon Island is shrouded in secrecy. The Herbiscus Confusus could be used as a dangerous weapon."

"So what has this got to do with the final trial?" asked Plato.

"The final trial is to climb down into the mouth of the volcano and return with a single flower from the plant," said Empress Me. "Jet, Turbold, you will be climbing down into one of nature's most destructive forces. You will be clinging on to volcanic rock, and battling against the steaming air currents. In short, it will be burning hot, uncomfortable, and extremely windy."

"Sounds like my experience with that viper vindaloo I ate in Varanasi," said Bruce.

"It sounds very dangerous," said Chuck seriously.

"We admit this task is not without danger," replied Empress Me. "Of course, either competitor is welcome to bow out at this stage."

"No way," said Jet and Turbold, speaking together.

"Very well," said Empress Me. "Then take your places."

Jet and Turbold stood at the edge of the crater and laid down their weapons. The others gathered around to watch.

"Good luck, Jet," called Donnie.

"Be careful," warned Chuck.

"The competitors are in place," said Empress Me. "Let the third and final trial commence."

Jet and Turbold bowed, then began to clamber down into the volcano. The lemurs on the slope applauded excitedly, and it wasn't long before Jet and Turbold had vanished from sight.

CHAPTER SEVEN

THE TRIAL OF THE VOLCANO

Turbold and Jet scrambled down quickly but carefully, aware that to lose their footing would be to lose their lives in the lava that bubbled in the pit of the crater. In spite of Turbold's natural skill as a climber, Jet was determined not to let him get the advantage. Both were darting in and out of caves as fast as they could in search of the plant, but the lower they got, the hotter it grew. The intense heat created sudden bursts of hot air that swirled around inside the volcano.

As Jet clung to the hot rock, he spotted a cluster of red petals fluttering out of one of the caves. But Turbold had spotted the petals too.

Meerkat and monkey clambered over to the cave as fast as they could manage, both reaching the plant at the same time.

"I beat you!" cried Turbold, plucking a red flower.

"Not if I get to the top before you!" replied Jet, grabbing a flower and scrambling to the mouth of the cave.

Now it was a race. The first to the top would be the winner. With victory in sight, they left the cave and began the long climb.

Up on top of the volcano, unable to see the drama unfolding within, Donnie was watching Stripes. The badger had turned his back to the others and was looking away from the volcano.

"What's he up to?" muttered Donnie, eyeing Stripes suspiciously.

"Do you think he's using his phone again?" asked Chuck.

Stripes turned back and saw them staring at him. He smiled and waved.

"Hey, look," said Bruce. "Someone's coming."

Everyone turned and saw a strange kind of car rumbling toward them, driving up the side of the volcano. It was bright yellow with purple spots. Circus music blasted out of speakers mounted on top.

Panic swept through the lemurs.

"We have intruders," cried Empress Me. "Stand strong, loyal subjects. They must not be allowed to disrupt the trial."

"That looks like an amphibious car," said Donnie. "It's a vehicle designed to travel on water and land. They must have sailed here from the mainland and then driven straight up the side of the volcano."

"But what is going on?" asked Plato.

"Look! It's the Ringmaster's circus goons," Chuck snarled. "What could those troublemakers be doing here? Where is their boss?"

"Let me at 'em," said Bruce, pushing his way down through the panicking lemurs. "I'll teach them to sneak up on us."

"Hardly sneaking though, is it?" said Donnie. "There's no way we could miss them."

As the vehicle rumbled closer, they could
see the knife-throwing Herr Flick and the
evil Von Trapeze family in the back. When it
finally came to a standstill, Doris the
Dancing Dog leaped down and grabbed leaf
masks from several lemurs, who were too
shocked to fight back. She ran back to the
circus goons with the masks.

"Hey, Grimsby," said Sheffield. "What
happens when a volcano loses its temper?"

"It blows its top," replied Grimsby, with
a sinister chuckle.

"What do you want?" demanded Bruce. "Because if it's a fight you're looking for, I'd say you're a bit outnumbered."

"Actually, *mein meerkatzchen*," Herr Flick said with a grin, "we've already done what we came to do. Our diversion has distracted you rather nicely."

Suddenly, a scream rang out from the top of the volcano. The meerkats spun around to see Stripes holding Empress Me, dangling her upside down over the edge of the crater, her hands bound.

"Let her go," cried Bruce.

"With pleasure," replied Stripes, pretending to let her drop but catching her before she plummeted down into the boiling lava. "One more step and I drop her for real."

"Why have you betrayed Empress Me's trust?" asked Chuck.

"For this," replied Stripes, holding up Empress Me's dried red flower.

"You mean you were in league with the Ringmaster all along?" asked Chuck.

"My first job was working in his circus—that's where I learned to juggle. I learned a lot more from the Ringmaster than I ever learned off my old dad. In fact, the only thing Dad ever taught me was the secret of Dragon Island."

"So you told the Ringmaster about the Herbiscus Confusus," said Chuck.

"I did indeed. I'm going to hand the plant over to the Ringmaster and there's nothing you can do to stop me!" cried Stripes. "If you try, the Empress will die!"

"This is all very well, but how exactly do you plan to get that flower off the island?" asked Donnie. "In case you haven't noticed, you're surrounded by the best fighters in the world, not to mention an army of lemurs."

Stripes glanced up. "Ah, right on time. *Here* is the answer to your question."

Over the crest of the volcano rose a hot-air balloon. In the basket below the red-and-white striped balloon stood a shadowy figure in a top hat.

"You cannot allow him to take the plant off this island," said Empress Me, sounding remarkably calm for one being held upside down over a fiery volcano.

Stripes shook her violently, making her scream out in fear. The Ringmaster brought the balloon overhead and let down a rope ladder.

"You won't get away with this, Ringmaster," yelled Chuck.

"I disagree, Chuck," the Ringmaster shouted in reply. "With this plant, I will create bombs of confusion. With these bombs I will throw the world into disarray. When it comes to its senses it will find it has a new master . . . The Ringmaster. Now, Stripes, drop the lemur, grab the ladder, and let's get going."

Stripes looked at the meerkats, shrugged, and released Empress Me's ankle, dropping her into the volcano.

"Nooo!" cried Chuck. He and Donnie leaped forward to the edge of the volcano, landing on their bellies, but they were not quite quick enough to catch Empress Me. Above their heads, Stripes was being lifted into the air by the balloon.

"We missed," said Donnie.

"Luckily we didn't," said a voice from inside the volcano.

Chuck and Donnie peered over the edge and saw Jet and Turbold holding Empress Me between them.

"Now, give us a hand, would you?" said Jet.

"Of course," replied Chuck. He and Donnie helped pull them to safety.

CHAPTER EIGHT

THE BATTLE OF DRAGON ISLAND

"Circus folk," cried the Ringmaster. "Let the mayhem commence!"

While the Ringmaster and Stripes rose into the sky in the balloon, down on the ground the clowns pulled a huge cannon out of the amphibious car. They fired at the rows of lemurs, who dived out of the way as red goo splattered on the ground.

"Hey, do you like our scalding hot jam gun?" yelled Grimsby.

"Yeah, now we're *really* jamming!" said Sheffield.

"And you'll all be toast," added Grimsby.
The lemurs were quick to retaliate and
began to attack the clowns using expert
kung-fu moves. But Herr Flick joined the
fight, throwing knives while the Von Trapeze
children engaged in somersaulting attacks.
The lemurs blocked and dodged but, never
having fought a real battle before, they
struggled against the circus goons.

"Listen to me, lemurs of Dragon Island,"
cried Chuck, holding his sword aloft. "Join
us, and we will lead you in battle. Before
the Clan each enemy cowers, for now we
fight till victory is ours."

"Let's show them whose island this is,"
said Bruce. With a cry of "Bruce Force!" he
charged forward. First he took Herr Flick
by surprise and, with a magnificent punch
to the chest, sent him reeling. Next, he

took on Doris the Dancing Dog. Bruce
dodged one of the dog's lunges and
clonked her on the back of her head. As
he was about to knock her out altogether,
he came under fire from the clown's jam
gun. Normally, having jam fired at him
would be Bruce's idea of a good time, but
the jam the clowns were using was so hot,
it sizzled. Bruce leaped out of the way, but
both clowns kept firing.

Suddenly, Lay-Z opened his eyes and sprang into action. He leaped up, soared over the lemurs' heads, and, with an outstretched claw, knocked Sheffield away from the cannon. Next, he triple somersaulted in the air and came down on the cannon, twisting the barrel and whacking Grimsby on the nose. Grimsby tried to fire at him but, with the barrel twisted, the gun backfired, covering his baggy pants with burning hot jam.

"Youch," he yelped, pulling off his pants to reveal a big pair of purple underwear.

The lemurs fell about laughing at this. With the clowns' jam gun out of action, Bruce led the lemurs in a forceful retaliation against the rest of the circus goons.

Meanwhile, Donnie hauled Empress Me to safety as Turbold and Jet climbed back up to the top of the volcano. Chuck turned to Plato. "We need to stop the Ringmaster getting away with the Herbiscus Confusus flower," he said. "Can you carry me up there?"

"It would be my pleasure," replied the pelican.

Chuck grabbed hold of his feet and Plato flew up toward the balloon.

"If you rip the fabric of the balloon with your beak, I'll drop down into the basket and get the plant," said Chuck.

"If I burst the balloon the basket will plummet," warned Plato.

"Let me worry about that," replied Chuck. "We need to stop the Ringmaster. He can't get away with this."

Neither the Ringmaster nor Stripes spotted the pelican or the meerkat until it was too late. Plato punctured the balloon with his beak and it rapidly began to lose height, swirling through the smoke as it fell.

Chuck landed on the edge of the basket, his sword drawn.

"Chuck Cobracrusher," snarled the Ringmaster. He cracked his whip at Chuck but he was too slow, and Chuck leaped over it. "You can't win, Ringmaster," Chuck said.

The balloon was sinking down toward the volcano.

"Stripes," yelled the Ringmaster. "Make yourself useful and knock this meddlesome meerkat into that volcano."

"My pleasure," replied Stripes.

Stripes aimed a powerful fist at Chuck, but he somersaulted out of the way and landed on the other side of the basket, leaving Stripes teetering on the edge.

"You hopeless badger," growled the Ringmaster, cracking his whip and sending Stripes over the side.

The badger fell with a cry of terror, but Plato swooped down and grabbed him before he reached the bubbling lava.

Chuck was perched on the edge of the basket, eye-to-eye with his enemy as they continued dropping down toward the smoking crater. Chuck was still wearing his

leaf mask but the Ringmaster had no way of avoiding the smoke.

"If you give me the flower, then we can both jump to safety," said Chuck.

The Ringmaster laughed maniacally. "Give it to you? I'll never give up this flower . . . although I can't remember why . . ."

"You have breathed the fumes," said Chuck. "You don't know what you're saying. You won't survive the volcano."

"I can survive anything! I am the . . . someone . . . I forget who . . ."

As the basket came level with the top of the crater, Chuck leaped to safety and the basket dropped down inside.

The Ringmaster's crazed laughter echoed around the inside of the crater, growing quieter and quieter until it could be heard no more. A great cloud of red smoke rose up.

At the mouth of the volcano, Jet, Turbold, and Donnie had joined the fight. Jet and Turbold were working as a team, taking it in turns to pummel the Von Trapeze family. Jet used his Super-charged Shock Attack to send sparks at the evil siblings while Turbold held them back.

Donnie pulled a missile from his bag, lit the fuse and sent it flying directly into the amphibious vehicle. Hundreds of lemurs cheered as the colorful vehicle exploded into pieces.

Even Empress Me was fighting, elegantly dodging a series of knives thrown by Herr Flick, then kicking his feet from under him. As he tumbled to the ground, countless lemurs leaped on his chest to pin him down.

"You've thrown your last knife on this island," said Empress Me to the distressed knife thrower.

e spun around to face the clowns. They realized they were surrounded by hundreds of angry-looking lemurs ready to fight.

"What time is it, Grimsby?" asked Sheffield.

"Half past time to get out of here, I'd say, Sheffield," replied Grimsby.

They turned and pushed their way through the wall of lemurs, who kicked, punched, and bit them as they fled down the slopes of the volcano.

"Wait for us!" yelled Herr Flick, running after the clowns. He was closely followed by the Von Trapeze family.

Doris stood at the edge of the volcano, looking for her master.

"Come on, Doris," yelled Grimsby.

But Doris didn't move—and then, all of a sudden, she disappeared into the volcano.

"What happened to the Ringmaster?" asked Bruce.

"He was still in the balloon when it fell. He refused to save himself," said Chuck.

"Congratulations, Clan of the Scorpion. You have finally defeated your enemy," said Empress Me.

"So it would seem," said Chuck.

"That's fantastic!" exclaimed Bruce.

"There is still one loose end to tie up," said Plato.

The pelican was hovering in the air, holding Stripes upside down.

"Let go of me," demanded Stripes, as he struggled to get free.

"Mr. Stripes," said Empress Me. "You have broken the sacred oath you swore. You betrayed us. You are no longer welcome on Dragon Island."

"You hear that?" said Plato. "Time for

a swim." He tossed the badger up into the air, then spun around and booted him so hard that he flew out to sea, landing in the distance with a great splash.

Back at the camp, the lemurs and the competitors gathered in the clearing.

"We must say this has been a most remarkable competition," Empress Me announced. "And now the time has come to award the title of Ultimate Dragon Warrior."

"But no one succeeded in the third task," said Turbold. "Neither of us got the flower to the top."

"This is true," replied Empress Me. "And that is why we have decided on an unusual result. This has indeed been a remarkable contest and it calls for a remarkable result. All of you fought admirably to protect the island, but there are four among you who shone out in our eyes. And therefore, for nobly leading our lemurs in battle, for

preventing the theft of the Herbiscus Confusus, and for finally defeating the Ringmaster, the Clan of the Scorpion are hereby *all* named the Ultimate Dragon Warriors."

"All of us?" said Jet.

"All of you," said Empress Me.

"Ninja-boom!" cried Jet.

Empress Me and the lemurs bowed, followed by Turbold, Plato, and Lay-Z.

"It is time for a celebration," said Empress Me.

"A celebration with food?" asked Bruce.

"Indeed," said Empress Me. She clapped her hands together. "We will now prepare a banquet fit for four Ultimate Dragon Warriors."

"That sounds great!" said Bruce. "What are the others going to have?"

GOFISH

Gareth P. Jones

What did you want to be when you grew up?
At various points, a writer, a musician, an intergalactic bounty hunter and, for a limited period, a graphic designer. (I didn't know what that meant, but I liked the way it sounded.)

When did you realize you wanted to be a writer?
I don't remember realizing it. I have always loved stories. From a very young age, I enjoyed making them up. As I'm not very good at making things up on the spot, this invariably involved having to write them down.

What's an embarrassing childhood memory?
Seriously? There are too many. I have spent my entire life saying and doing embarrassing things. Just thinking about some of them is making me cringe. Luckily, I have a terrible memory, so I can't remember them all, but no, I'm not going to write any down for you. If I did that, I'd never be able to forget them.

What's your favorite childhood memory?
To be honest with you, I don't remember my childhood very well at all (I told you I had a bad memory), but I do recall how my dad used to tell me stories. He would make them up as he went along, most likely borrowing all sorts of elements from the books he was reading without me knowing.

As a young person, who did you look up to most?
My mom and dad, Prince, Michael Jackson, all of Monty Python, and Stephen Fry.

What was your favorite thing about school?
Laughing with my friends.

What was your least favorite thing about school?
I had a bit of a hard time when I moved from the Midlands to London at the age of twelve because I had a funny accent. But don't worry, it was all right in the end.

What were your hobbies as a kid? What are your hobbies now?
I love listening to and making music. My hobbies haven't really changed over the years, except that there's a longer list of instruments now. When I get a chance, I like idling away the day playing trumpet, guitar, banjo, ukulele, mandolin (and piano if there's one in the vicinity). I also like playing out with my friends.

What was your first job, and what was your "worst" job?

My first job was working as a waiter. That's probably my worst job, too. As my dad says, I was a remarkably grumpy waiter. I'm not big on all that serving-people malarkey.

What book is on your nightstand now?

I have a pile of books from my new publisher. I'm trying to get through them before I meet the authors. I'm half-way through *Maggot Moon* by Sally Gardner, which is written in the amazing voice of a dyslexic boy.

How did you celebrate publishing your first book?

The first time I saw one of my books in a shop, I was so excited that I caused something of a commotion. I managed to persuade an unsuspecting customer to buy it so I could sign it for her son.

Where do you write your books?

Anywhere and everywhere. Here are some of the locations I have written the Ninja Meerkats series: On the 185 and the 176 buses in London, various airplanes, Hong Kong, Melbourne, all over New Zealand, a number of cafes and bars between San Diego and San Francisco, New Quay in South Wales, and my kitchen.

What sparked your imagination for the Ninja Meerkats?

The idea came from the publishing house, but from the moment I heard it, I really wanted to write it. It reminded me of lots of action-packed cartoons I used to watch when I was young. I love the fact that I get to cram in lots of jokes and puns, fast action, and crazy outlandish plots.

The Ninja Meerkats are awesome fighters; have you ever studied martial arts? If so, what types?
Ha, no. If I was to get into a fight, my tactic would be to fall over and hope that whoever was attacking me lost interest.

If you were a Ninja Meerkat, what would your name be?
Hmm, how about Gareth *POW!* Jones?

What's your favorite exhibit or animal at the zoo?
Funnily enough, I like the meerkats. I was at a zoo watching them the other day when it started to rain. They suddenly ran for cover, looking exactly like their human visitors.

What's Bruce's favorite food?
Anything with the words ALL YOU CAN EAT written above it.

If you had a catchphrase like Bruce Force! or Ninja-Boom! what would it be?
That's a tricky one. How about PEN POWER!

If you were a Ninja Meerkat, what would your special ninja skill be?
I like to think I'd be like Jet, and always working on a new skill. When I got into school, I took the Random Move

Generator! We used it to come up with new moves, like the Floating Butterfly Punch and the Ultimate Lemon Punch.

What is your favorite thing about real-life meerkats? Have you ever met a meerkat?
I was lucky enough to go into a meerkat enclosure recently. They were crawling all over me, trying to get a good view. It was brilliant.

What challenges do you face in the writing process, and how do you overcome them?
The challenge with writing the Ninja Meerkats books is mostly about the plotting. It's trying to get all the twists and turns to work, and to avoid them feeling predictable. When I hit problems, I write down as many options as I can think of from the completely ordinary to utterly ridiculous. Once they're all down on paper, the right answer normally jumps out at me.

Which of your characters is most like you?
I'd like to say that I'm wise and noble like Chuck, but I'm probably more like the Ringmaster as we're both always coming up with new ways to take over the world.

What makes you laugh out loud?
My friends.

What do you do on a rainy day?
Play guitar, write, watch TV, or go out with my sword-handled umbrella.

What's your idea of fun?
Answering questionnaires about myself. Actually, tomorrow, I'm going to a music festival with my wife where we will dance and cavort. That should be fun.

What's your favorite song?
There are far too many to mention, but today I think I'll go for "Feel Good Inc." by Gorillaz.

Who is your favorite fictional character?
Another tricky one, but today I'll say Ged from the Earthsea Trilogy by Ursula K. Le Guin.

What was your favorite book when you were a kid?
As a child, I especially loved *The Phantom Tollbooth* by Norton Juster.

What's your favorite TV show or movie?
Raiders of the Lost Ark.

If you were stranded on a desert island, who would you want for company?
My wife and son, then probably my friend Pete, as he's really handy and would be able to make and build things.

If you could travel anywhere in the world, where would you go and what would you do?
I'd like to go to Canada next. Ideally, I'd like to go and live there for a bit. I've never been to South America. There are also lots of parts of America I haven't visited yet.

If you could travel in time, where would you go and what would you do?
I think I'd travel to the future and see what's changed and whether anyone's invented a new kind of umbrella.

What's the best advice you have ever received about writing?
Don't tell the story, show the story.

What advice do you wish someone had given you when you were younger?
Everything's probably going to be fine, so it's best to enjoy yourself.

Do you ever get writer's block? What do you do to get back on track?
It feels like tempting fate, but I don't really believe in writer's block. I think if you can't write, you're doing the wrong thing. You may need to plan or jot down options or go for a walk.

What do you want readers to remember about your books?
I'd settle for a general feeling of having enjoyed them.

What would you do if you ever stopped writing?
I'd do a full stop. If this is for an American audience, I guess that would be a period.

What should people know about you?
I'm a very silly man.

SQUARE FISH

The Clan head down under to investigate strange
reports from the Australian outback.
Is the Ringmaster up to his old tricks?

Killer koalas and kangaroos are no match for the
Meerkats in **OUTBACK ATTACK**.

Ninja-Boom!

CHAPTER ONE

BELLA WILLOWHAMMER

Bathed in the warm glow of the morning sun, the world-famous Sydney Opera House looked like it was made out of segments of a gigantic orange. Hidden between two of those segments were four ninja meerkats.

Donnie Dragonjab put away the grappling hook they had used to climb up there. "I wonder why your sister chose this as a meeting point, Bruce," he said.

"Search me," said Bruce. "But she definitely said in her e-mail to meet on the roof of the Opera House."

"I expect Bella chose it because it is discreet and yet easy to find for first-time visitors to Sydney," said Chuck.

"Who's this Sydney you keep talking about?" asked Bruce.

"Sydney is the name of the city, Bruce," said Jet.

"Oh yeah," replied Bruce, scratching his head.

"I'm amazed a sister of yours even knows how to send an e-mail," said Donnie. "The last time you tried to use the computer, you smashed it to pieces."

"You were the one who told me to boot it," protested Bruce.

"I said *re*boot it," replied Donnie.

"Yeah, well, Bella was always the smart Willowhammer," admitted Bruce.

"What does she do here in Australia?" asked Chuck.

"I don't know."

"I hope it's something exciting," said Jet. "Life's been so boring since we defeated our enemy, the Ringmaster."

"As followers of the Way of the Scorpion, we should not seek excitement and adventure," said Chuck.

"Yeah, but since he's gone, the closest we've had to some action was when Bruce thought that someone had stolen his packet of pickled newts' knees."

"It didn't take long to solve that one, did it, Bruce?" said Donnie pointedly.

"I told you, I forgot I ate them," said Bruce.

"The point is that since Chuck pushed the Ringmaster into the volcano on Dragon Island, everything has been as dull as dishwater," complained Jet.

"Now Jet, you know perfectly well I did not push the Ringmaster into that volcano," said Chuck. "I tried to stop him, but he had already become hopelessly confused by inhaling the red fumes of the Herbiscus Confusus."

"All I know is that this mission had better involve some real fighting," said Jet. "I'm itching to practice my new Australian-style moves. Who wants to see

my Counter-clockwise Clonk or my Upside-
down Punch?"

"I do like a meerkat who knows his
moves," said a female voice.

The Clan of the Scorpion spun around,
but they were unable to see where the voice
had come from, until a meerkat appeared,
apparently out of thin air. Bella Willowhammer
landed in front of them and smiled. She wore
a brimmed hat, an overcoat, and a satchel
over her shoulder.

"Sissy!" exclaimed Bruce, grabbing hold of her and giving her a big hug.

"Hello, Bruce," said Bella, gasping for breath.

"Miss Willowhammer, I am pleased to meet you. I'm Chuck Cobracrusher," said Chuck, solemnly bowing.

"The name's Jet Flashfeet," said Jet, shaking her paw.

"How did you jump out of thin air like that?" demanded Donnie.

"And you must be Donnie Dragonjab," said Bella. "In answer to your question, my sudden appearance is down to this little beauty." She pressed a button on her coat collar, and a strange flying object came down from above and landed next to her. It had a circular base with a long pole in the center and propellers on top.

"Cool flying machine!" said Jet.

"Nice design," said Donnie. "But how was it invisible?"

"It wasn't," replied Bella. "The base is painted the same color as the sky. This makes it impossible to see from below, which means that it's a perfect vehicle for getting around the city unnoticed. I call it the Bella-copter."

"Bella, we are all intrigued as to why you have summoned us," said Chuck.

"I work as a private detective here in Sydney," she replied, "and I need your help. Recently I was hired by a scientist called Professor Bill Abong. He's an expert in rare plants. He sounded all jittery on the phone. He kept saying he thought he was being followed. I told him to call the police, but he'd already tried them. They laughed him out of the station."

"Why?" asked Bruce.

"He believed he was being followed by koalas."

"Koalas? You mean those cute cuddly teddy-bear things?" said Bruce.

"That cuddly stuff is just a front," said Bella. "The League of Extreme Koalas have a claw in every crime in the city."

"And were they following this scientist?" asked Chuck.

"Yes. They were watching him and I was

watching them. But they must have spotted me, because while I was keeping an eye on the professor's house late at night, they attacked me and knocked me out. When I came round, the professor had been kidnapped. So, you see, I need your help to rescue him. These koalas can be pretty rough, and I need some real fighters on my side."

"Then the Clan of the Scorpion is at your disposal," said Chuck.

"Now this sounds like a real adventure," added Jet.